Don R. Frazer

The Irish volunteer

Don R. Frazer

The Irish volunteer

ISBN/EAN: 9783744741071

Printed in Europe, USA, Canada, Australia, Japan

Cover: Foto ©Andreas Hilbeck / pixelio.de

More available books at **www.hansebooks.com**

THE IRISH VOLUNTEER.

A Drama of the

War OF THE Rebellion.

BY DON R. FRAZER,

92nd Ill. Mtd Infantry.

Presented in Cole's Opera House, Mount Carroll, Ill., March, 1885, with the following cast of characters:

PADDY CARNEY, The Irish Volunteer, -	W. H. WILDEY.
CAPT. DENTON, Federal, - -	J. W. CORMANY.
MR. ALDINE, - - -	E. T. E. BECKER.
CHARLIE ALDINE, } - -	FRANK HUGHES. JOHN SQUIRES.
FEDERAL SOLDIERS, ETC., -	NASE POST NO. 80, G. A. R.
CAPT. CRANDON, Confederate, -	C. C. FARMER.
STANFORD, a Guerrilla, - -	DON R. FRAZER.
CAPT. HILL, - - -	W. D. HUGHES.
JORDAN, a Scout, - - -	W. P. ROBBE.
CONFEDERATE SOLDIERS, -	NASE POST NO. 80.
MARION KINGSLEY, - -	ESTELLA HEWITT.
MRS. ALDINE, - -	KATE ROSENSTOCK.
ETHEL ALDINE, - -	JEAN A. HUGHES.

CAL M. FEEZER, STAGE MANAGER.

THE IRISH VOLUNTEER.

ACT I.—Scene 1. Chamber.

(Recruiting officer at table—Men standing about.)

Off.—Who is next?   (Char. approaches.)

Off—You are too young my boy; I am afraid you can't go.

Char.—I want to go as a drummer if I can't carry a gun.

O—Can you beat the drum?

Ch—I can sir.

O—What does your parents say about it?

Ch—They do not wish me to go sir, but I can't stay at home.

Off—Where is your father?

Mr. A—I am the lad's father, captain; I am opposed to his going, on account of his youth, but he seems to have set his heart on it and I am at a loss what to do.

Ch—Let me try it anyway, for a time.

Capt. Denton—These are recruits for my company, Mr. Aldine, and Charlie would be with me. I will have a care of the lad as far as it is in my power. I will not urge you to let him go, but I will keep him with me if he does go.

Mr A—Thank you, captain; if he is to go I would rather that he be with you than any one else. I know you will care for the lad. His mother must be consulted however: he is our baby; one of his brothers fell at Shiloh, the other is with Rosecrans; if harm should come to the boy it would break his mother's heart.

Off—Captain how soon will you be ready to start?

Capt D—I can be ready at any moment.

Off—Well then boys, day after to-morrow, you will meet

Capt Denton here, ready to go to the front with him. In the meantime, this young man will have an opportunity to obtain his mother's consent, and if it is obtained he can be mustered in when he gets to the regiment. You may go now.

(Enter Paddy Carney.)

Pad —Hould an! Hould an! It's meself thats goin till the wor. I'm frum the bogs af Killarney be dad, an me name is Paddy Carney. Pit me down Gineral. I'm under 18 and over 45; I'm tin fate lang an tree feet wide; I weigh twinty stun an feel loike a Rosicrusian: pit me down an giv me a cannin. Ah! Woosh! (Walks about flourishing shillalah.) Bring an your ribils. I kin kill an ate a dozen av thim as aisy as if they wis shmelts. Hooray fur Ould Ireland furiver an down wid the dirty shpalpanes that insoolts the shtars an sthripes. Hooray fur fitin an divarshuns!

Off—Do you want to enlist, my man?

Paddy—Enlisht! Phats that now!

Off—Why, to join the army and go to war.

Paddy—Ay, that I do. Go to war! Give me a clare field an no favor an be dad I'll shpoil the noses av a schore av them. It its fitin ye want me b'y, its the loikes av Paddy Carney ye'll be wantin' to do it, be loike. Pit me down, I say. Hooray.

Off—All right, Paddy, out you go.

Paddy—Who said out ye go? Be dad thry it! Its not out I'll go, an yez can't pit me out, ye murtherin thafe av the wurruld. Come outsoide an pit me out wunce.

Off—I meant you should go out to the front with the boys.

Paddy—O, did ye. Thin out I'll go, an be dad if I live to I die, if I don't hev lashins av divarshun ye may take me nose fur a fog horn.

Off—Well boys, let us sing a rallying song before we go, and don't forget to meet me here day after to-morrow at noon.

Paddy—We'll be on hand. Captin, loike a sore thumb.

(Song—Rally 'Round the Flag.)   (Drill)

SCENE 2.—IN THE WOODS.

Paddy—I'd giv noine dollars to know pwhere I am be dad, Wait to I figger a bit. Foorst, I'm in the Confiderate states. Am I, be dad! Thin by the piper that played before Moses, I'm not. Divil the bit is there any Confiderit states. This is the iverlastin glorious Union foriver, and down wid the traitors an oop wid the shtars; so sez I, Paddy Carney, be dad. An so, if its in the Unitid States I àm, thin I'm all right. Secondly and thirdly, I'm in the state av Georgia. I wuz whin I shtarted onyhow, an as I hev'nt got to where I'm goin', thin I'm there yit. Thirdly an fourthly, I'm—losht, de dad Am I! Shure I'm not, fur I'm here. Well this is a divil av a pickle. I'm losht accordin to figgers an I'm not accordin to sinse. Paddy, me b'y yer aloive onyhow, an pwhats the odds. I'll jist hev a shmoke an a bit av divarshun bedad. (Voices in the distance.) Ay! Phats that? Be the powers av the two tailed Kilkenny cats, somebody's goin to distoorb me drames, an fur fear I'll be in the way I'll jist shlide behint this big dornick.　　　　(Hides behind rock.)

　　　　　　　　Enter Cran. and Stan. R.

Stan—I tell you Captain, if you are bound to go to the devil to see a girl, you will have to go alone. I'll be shot if you can get me to run my neck into a noose to pilot you through thirty miles o' Yankee scouts and pickets. You hav'nr gold enough to tempt me.

Cran—I don't want you to pilot me. You have been through there several times since the Yankees came into the valley and ought to know something about how they are located. All I want is for you to tell me where their pickets are. I'll manage the rest.

Stan—Tell you where they are! They are like Pharaoh's locusts; they're everywhere. And wherever they are not, their scouts swarm like flies. I got enough of it the last time, and if I had not been certain of being taken if I remained, I never would have tried to get through.

Cran—Well, well, if you got through safely, why cannot I? I am going if the whole Yankee army was in the valley. I shall be able to outwit them without difficulty.

Paddy—(Looking over rock.) O, wull ye be dad.

Stan—What's that! I thought I heard a voice close by.

Cran—Well, what if you did; are you afraid of a voice? It seems to me that your late experience has destroyed your nerve slightly.

Stan—My late experience has made me suspicious of even the shaking of a leaf and I expect to see a Yankee behind every tree. You will feel that way too, Captain, by the time you get back, if you do get back.

Cran—O, never fear, I'll get back without difficulty. But I intend finding out what the Yankees are doing before I come back

Paddy—[Aside]—O, now, wull ye be dad.

Stan.—You will need to look pretty sharp. I think you will find as smart fellows among those Yankees as you will find any where. I have been among them.

Cran—Smart! Greasy mechanics, mudsills and farmer's boys. Why I could go through their camp in broad day and they would never suspect that I was a follower of the 'Bonnie Blue Flag.'

Stan—If you will take my advice, Captain, you will not try that. Foolhardiness is not courage by any means and if you think that the Yankees go about with their eyes shut, you will wake up some morning with your neck in a noose. Take my advice and don't presume on the dullness of the Federal troops.

Cran—Faugh! Keep your advice for fellows who will take it. I am going up the valley if I swing for it and I am going to start to-night. I have leave of absence for four weeks and if I am not back in that time you may conclude that Capt. Crandon has embellished an oak.

Stan—Well, have a care, Captain. Hope you'll get through safely, but you are taking alarming chances.

Cran—Good day; meet me here at 8 o'clock this evening.

Stan—I'll be here.   (Exit Stan and Cran.)

Pad—(Coming from behind rock.) So'll I, be dad.   An ain't he a foin wan, that Captin'.   Be dad if there was ony tree av such chaps they wid kill an ate the intcire Union Army in liss than a month.   O be gorra, I'm av the opinun that the yung gintleman will hev a bit av a dance up the valley an its Paddy Carney that'll play the fiddle till the dancin'.   I'll jis take the trouble to kape my oye an that majir gineril, be dad.   I 'll take a bit av walk after him. (Starts L   Enter Stan. R.)

Stan—Halt !'   'Bout face.   Can't you turn your body?

P—I can, sor.

Stan—Why don't you then?

P—Be dad an yez told me to bout face.

Stan—'Bout your body then.

P—Be dad, an what fur thin?

Stan—Turn around here I tell you.

P—Go to the divil an turn me around yersilf.   (S does so.)

Stan—Well, who in blazes are you, and what are you doing here?

P—I'm the divil, an I'm standin' here.

Stan—O, you are the devil are you; when did you come up?

P—I'm alwis up at prisint.   I heard a while ago that there wus a wa-ar goin on here an I cum up to enjoy the divarshun.

Stan—Well, this is the first time I knew the devil was an Irishman.

P—An its many things that mabbe yez don't know yit, me foine felly.   Pit down that crooked stick yez hev in yer hand, or I'll swally it.

Stan—I think that if you 'swallied' it you might get blown up with it.

P.—Its not up I want to go: be dad.   Now, phwat are yez doin here yersilf, me foine felly.   Yez take great liberty wid me axin so many questions.   Who are yez, onyhow?

Stan—My name is Stanford, I'm a Confederate soldier.

P—O, yez are. So yez is wun av thim fellys that are up to drinkin' blood and raisin such a hullaballoo an the arth at prisint. An how many more av yez fellys is there about here, may I hev the obligeness to ax?

Stan—Only about 3,000, and they are going away shortly.

P—Are yez wan av the big fellys or ony a shmall wan?

Stan—I'm what they call a guerrilla. I come and go where I please, and take orders from nobody.

P—A gorilla! Then yez is wan av the fellys that take a crack at the b'ys from behint the trees an sich. Yez look loike it. Be dad if there was more av our family I'd think yez wus me twin brother. Yez wud make a foin divil, so yez wud.

Stan—Well, my friend, I think I'll take you to camp and exhibit you to the boys up there.

P—O, wull yez, now. Whin, be dad?

Stan—Now. Come along. (Turns to walk away, when P' whips out a couple revolvers)

P—Shtap! (Stan. turns about.) I'll throuble yez to toss that crooked iron over this way; I want to swally it. (S. does so.) Have yez ony more av thim things about yer close?

Stan—No; that's all.

P—Now me foine felly, I'll throuble yez to pit yer whrist in this little fixen. (Produces handcuffs. Stan. hesitates. P raises revolver. S. puts hand in.) Now the other. (Stan. puts in the other.) Now, be dad, yez'll go wid me wance. Come into the woods a bit, I want to have a chat wid yez. [Exit L.]

[Enter Crandon, R.]

Cran—It is after eight o'clock and Stanford should be here. I wonder where he can be. I should be away by this time. He thinks my trip up the valley is a dangerous one, but love laughs at locksmiths and Yankee pickets, so I am going through. It has been a year since I saw Marion, and the time has seemed an age. My coming will be a surprise to her, and although she is devoted to the Union and the old flag, I hope to convince her that the South is in the right and will soon achieve her independence. Then we will have a nation of gentlemen.

[Enter Paddy, L.

P—O, now, wull yez, be dad. (C. turns, faces P's pistol.) Good avenin' sor. Don't wink or be dad I'll sind yez to glory by the lead mine route. (produces handcuffs.) Wull yez be so koin : as to obligate me by puttin' yer fisht in this little bit av iern?

Cran—No, never ! I'll die first.

P—Be dad that'll suit me to a dot. Yez won't be givin me anny throuble, thin. Hev yez onything to say before ye die foorst.

Cran—No ! Shoot ! shoot, you infernal assassin !

P—Divil the sassin am I, but I've got a timper loike foire an I'm gittin purty hot, avick, an if yez hev ony word to sind to yer Marion, yez better shpit it out an I'll tell her. Its me that'll see her in a few days.

Cran—Do you know her?

P.--Put yer hand in there or ye'll get a bullet in a howly second. (C. handcuffed.) Now thin, me foine felly, yer all right an ye'll obligate me greatly if ye'll shtop here a minit, I want to introjuce a friend till yez. (Exit and return with Stan.) Now Captin Crandon I hev the owdashous obligation av presintin to yez the gintlemanly cutthroat an robber, the gorilla Stanford. Mebby yez hev met him before.

Cran—Well, Stanford, you seem to be in the same predicament that I am. How did it happen?

Stan—I took this cursed Yank for a fool and he got the drop on me.

Cran—He took me in the same way.

Stan—Well, we seem to be in for it unless some of our men happen along this way pretty soon.

Cran—Keep your eyes open. We must find some way to outwit this infernal Irishman.

P—Well byes, phat div yez think av it onyway? Yer a couple of foine wans entoirely, an't yez? I belave I'll git the whole ribel army if I kape an.   But I can't fool wid yez much longer. Ive got to get out av this. (Soliloquises) Be dad I don't know phwat to do wid de shpalpanes. I don't want to murther thim and I can't take thim wid me an I can't let thim go. Be jabers, I hev it; I'll tie the divils togedder and tie thim till a tree. It'll be foine divarshun. (Approaches.) Well, byes, I musht lave yez fur the prisint and I'll be under the paneful necessity av lavin yez here. I'm goin to tackle yez togedder an lave yez tied till a tree.

Cran—You infernal scoundrel, do you intend to leave us to starve?

P—No, honey, but yez'll hev to take yer chances av somebody's findin yez before yez git that fur alang. Jist shtep this way, gintlemen. (Paddy unfastens one wrist of each, fastens them together and starts to lead them off, when they knock him down, search his pockets for key, unlock handcuffs aud pinion P) Phwat the divil med that tree fall on me hed. (Sees handcuffs.) O, wurra! wurra! an is it Paddy Carney that is caught in the darbies! Ohone! ohone! that I should live to see it.

Stan—Get up here, you sneaking Yankee spy ! What's to hinder me from blowing your brains out.

P—I hav'nt got any brains. If I had, be dad, I wouldn't be here like a bear in a trap.

Cran—Well, you won't be here long. Let us take him to camp and turn him over to the Colonel; they can try him and hang him for a spy

P—(Aside.) O, wull yez, be dad.   [Exit R.]

SCENE 3.—COURT MARTIAL.

Judge Advocate seated at table, others seated around.

J. A—Bring in the prisoner. (Enter P. guarded. Charge read.) What do you say, guilty or not guilty.

P—Phwat?

J. A—Are you guilty or not guilty?

P—Am I guilty or not guilty of phwat, be dad?

J. A—You are charged with being a spy from the Federal army.

P—Is that so? Well, phwat did I spy?

J. A—You are here to answer, not to ask questions.

P—O, am I then. Well drive an wid yer ducks.

J. A—Answer my question. Are you guilty or not guilty?

P—Be dad, sor, I can't say, till I hear the ividence.

J. A—He refuses to plead. Enter a plea of not guilty.

P—I'm obligated to yez, sor, an if yez say its not guilty I am, thin be dad I'll be biddin yez good day sor. (Starts to go.)

J. A—Not so fast my friend, we are not through with you.

P—Yer not? Didn't yez say I was not guilty? Phwat is yez goin to thry me fur if I'm not guilty?

J. A—That is a legal technicality. Call the witnesses.

P—O, is it then. A touchnecality. O yer a quare set.

J. A—Capt. Crandon, you may tell the court what you know about this man being found in our lines in disguise.

Cran—Stanford and myself found this man about a mile from camp, arrested and brought him in. He was dressed as he is now and was armed with two revolvers, which we took from him, as well as two pairs of handcuffs. He could give no account of himself, but from his talk we take him to be a Yankee spy.

P—Yez lie; I'm a Frinchman, be dad.

J. A—Stanford tell the court what you know about the matter.

Stan—Capt Crandon has related all there is to it. We were together at the time. He told me that he was the devil, but I believe that he is a spy.

J. A—Prisoner, have you anything to say?

P—I hev, yer anner, if yez'll give me time.

J. A—O, yes, take all the time you want.

P—Well then, I'll wait till doomsday.

J. A—We can't wait that long. Any reasonable time, however.

P—Well thin, how wid Christmas two years suit yez.

J. A.—This is a serious matter and we permit no levity. You must say what you wish to say at once.

P—Be dad yer a quare set. Yez tell me to take me own time an thin tell me I musht spake at wance. To the divil wid yez.

J. A—Where are you from?

P—I'm frum Killarney. sor, an I wish I was frum here..

J. A—Where do you belong at present?

P—Its mighty ivident that I belong here at prisent, but be cad I'll not be long here if yez let me lave.

J. A—Do you belong to the Federal army?

P—Phwat if I do; can't a felly belang there if he wants to?

J. A—If you do, what are you doing here?

P—I'm tied here answerin yer fool questions.

J. A—Are you a Federal soldier?

P—Do I look loike wan? Or mabby yez never wis near enough to one to see phwat they look loike. Be dad they'd frighten the soul out av yez.

J. A—Your a fool.

P—If yez burn me for a fool, ye'll git mighty wise ashes, me b'y.

J. A—Guards, remove the prisoner.

P—Be dad yez naden't; I kin walk. (Exit R.)

J. A—Gentlemen, the proof is before you, what do you say? A ballot will be taken upon the guilt or innocence of the prisoner. (Ballot.) The court finds the prisoner guilty. A further ballot will be taken upon his punishment. (Ballot.) The court sentences the prisoner to death by hanging. Bring him in, (Enter P. and guard.) Prisoner, the court after due deliberation, finds you guilty of being a spy and sentences you to death by hanging. The time fixed for your execution is to-morrow at 4 o'clock in the afternoon. Remove the prisoner.

P—Hould an yez bloody villains. Phwat div yez mane by tellin me that I'm to be hung to-morra before a clock. Dlv yez think I loike the chokin well enough to take it for a divarshun?

J. A.—You had better prepare for death; your time is short.

P O, is it thin. Be the powers of Moll Kelly, it'll be lang enough for me to fix some av yez before I've done wid yez Ye tell me that ye hev thried me an after jue deliberation ye hev found me guilty av bein a sphy. Yez could hev found me guilty of murther jist as aisy. Yez wid hang an unwaned babby if yez thought it belanged to the Union army. (To Crandon.) Mabby ye'll take that thrip yez were spaking av, but may the ould Harry catch me neck if I don't be there before yez an shpoil some av yer fun. Hooray fur Ould Ireland an down wid the traitors an oop wid the shtars.

J. A—Will you join the Confederate army if we let you off?

P—Out wid yez, ye villain ! I wid hang a thousand years an die a thousand times before I'd folly the dirty rag yez call the Bonnie Blue Flag. Down wid it sez I, an down wid the traitors an villains that folly it. I kim from Ould Ireland to be a free man an I'll niver folly the thing that floats alongside av the whip that yez uses an yer nagurs. Down wid yer flag an yer whip ! I'll shwing bafore I'll uphold aither. (Tableau. Curtain.

ACT II.—Scene 1. Guard House.

Paddy handcuffed; guard marching; Paddy removes handcuffs
and as guard turns his back, springs up and seizes him by
the neck from behind; struggle, guard sinks down.

P—Be the howly poker that's a good job of garrotin, an
I'm av the opinun that the hangin won't come off to-morra.
Paddy Carney won't be there onyhow. The bloody ribils didn't
know that I had a bit av a shpring in the darbies that didn't nade
a kay to unlock thim. What divarshun! I think I'll fix this
Johnny sos he won't be givin ony throuble for a while. (Binds
and gags guard.) There now, me foine felly, I hope yez'll be
comfortable loike for a couple av hours, an by the same token I'll
take yer contraptions wid me. (Exit L. Enter relief g'd R.)

Off—Here's the prisoner, but where's the guard. (Soldier
turns guard over.)

Gd—This is the guard, but where's the prisoner?

Off—Give the alarm there one of you. Take off the gag
and unbind him. How did this happen? Where is your prisoner?

Gd—That devil of an Irishman got his handcuffs off and
choked me. While I was unconscious he bound me and got
away.

Off—This is a fine business. How long has he been gone?

Gd—Nearly two hours; he is miles away by this time.

Off—Go back to your quarters. I must report this to the
Colonel. There will be the very duce to pay. (Exit all, R.)

SCENE 2.—IN THE WOODS.

P—I wonder if they're hangin poor Paddy Carney to-day? Be dad bnt they musht hev hed some foine divarshun whin they found that the illigent gintlemon to be hung wasn't there. Now I'll see phwat that foine Captin is doin up the valley, an if I don't give him a shtart me name isn't Paddy Carney. Be dad, phwat divarshun. (Exit R.

SCENE 3.—FEDERAL CAMP. SOLDIERS LYING ABOUT.

P—I tell yez, b'ys, them ribs giv me a puty close shave an if it hadn't been fur me divarshun sure they'd pulled me neck. Troth, but sorra I am that I hed to lave me darbies, and the bloody tiefs stole me revolvers. But Uncle Sam's rich. I can get anither pair, if I have money enough.

Corp. Johnson—What are they going to do down there?

P—Goin to do? Break their bloody necks runnin away if we make a lick in that direction.

Corp J.—Will they fight?

P.—Foight? Sorra the bit. They's the crack fellys on fut racin an it would take a quarter horse to head wan av thim aff, if he got sight av the blue coats.

Corp J—Theu you think yur chances for getting a crack at them are rather slim?

P—If we do, b'ys, we'll hev to surprise them. If they found we wuz after them they'd be like Paddy's flea—when you get him under your thumb, be dad he ant there.

Corp. J.— Do you suppose you could find the place again?

P—Find it? Wid me two eyes shut a rod I could. Sure

I thought I'd never git out av the divil's nist, an I tuk a good luk at it. (Enter Crandon R. disguised.) [P. aside.] Be the howly poker that's him.

Cran---Well, boys, you seem to be enjoying yourselves. What regiment is this?

Corp. J---The 18th Infantry.

Cran--Whose brigade?

Corp. J---Col. Corcoran is in command. He is the Colonel of our regiment.

Cran---Ah, yes. Where is his headquarters?

Corp. J---About a mile up this way. What is your regiment.

Cran---I'm an aide-de-camp of General Dashwood, commanding 3d brigade, and am going up to headquarters to see some friends.

P—(Aside.) O, wull yez, be dad.

Cran---I hear we are going to move to the front in a few days. Have you heard anything about it in your regiment?

Corp. J.---No, but I wish we would move. We are getting tired of lying in camp. We may get a chance to have a brush with the brigade of Johnnies that are lying down the valley about thirty miles.

P—Whisht ! ye spalpane.

Cran---(Aside.) Good God! It's him and I'm lost.

P—Phwat's the matter wid yez. Yer taken quite pale like all to wance.

Cran---O, nothing, only I have a bad tooth ache; it makes me jump sometimes.

P—Better come wid me to the doctor's and hev it pulled sor.

Cran—O no, not now. It will ease up presently, I hope.

P—Where did yez scy yer brigade was, sor? I hev a cozin in wan av thim companies, Paddy Carney by name. Mabby ye know him, sor. He's a broth of a by, is Pat.

Cran—Yes, I know Pat. I have seen him around head

quarters several times. He looks very much like yourself.
(Aside.) Thank heaven, this is another Irishman.

P—Yes sor, its twins we are. Our mothers wuz sisters,
an I looked so much loike him that they called me Pat, afther
him, an then they named him Pat afther me. Pat's a great lad.
I heard he wis doin some scoutin among the Johnnies.

Cran—Yes, he is doing duty of that kind at present, I be
lieve. He has been on a scout for the last week or so and is
gone over his time. The Colonel is a little anxious about him.

P---(Aside.) Is he, be dad? O, yer a slick wan. (Aloud.)
Niver mind Pat. If they catch him it'll take a regiment to hould
him. I'll bet noine dollars that ye'll see Paddy Carney before
two days, sor.

Cran—(Aside.) I don't like this. There can't be two
men so exactly alike. (Aloud.) Well boys, good day, I'll walk
up to the Colonel's tent.

P---Tell Pat whin yez say him that his twin cousin is to
the fore yit. [Exit Cran. R. Paddy springs to his feet.] Be
the piper that played before Moses, its him ! An its great divarshun we'll hev. If we don't hev a hangin then I'm a Dutchman!

Corp. J---What's the matter with you Pat?

P---Phwats the matter wid me? Be jabers ! nothin's the
matter wid me, but there'll be somethin the matter wid somebody
before long. Tare an 'ouns but the bloody tief has got the
cheek to do phwat he tould dat murtherin gorilla he wid do.
O, thunder an turf, phwat cheek the felly has.

Corp. J---Pat, you're going crazy. What in thunder are
you talking about?

P---Oho, wasn't that a divarshun about me twin cozin?
Hooray ! Pat, yer a juel ! Heads I win; tails, yez lose ! Bedad
its the captain I want to say in a jiffy ! Corporal, if yez want
tree stripes on yer arrum kape yer oye an that chap fur two
minits. Don't let him pass the pickets.

Corp---What for, you crazy Irishman?

P---Yez'll find out in a jiffy. Do phwat I tell yez an yer a sargint to-morra. I'm off to find the captin. (Exit L.)

Corp---There's something wrong about that aide-de-camp or Pat wouldn't be so excited. Boys, let's follow the fellow and see whats in the wind. (Exit soldiers L.)

SCENE 4.---A PICKET GUARD.

Enter Crandon hurriedly.

Guard—Halt.

Cran—I'm an aide-de-camp on General Dashwood's staff and on urgent business. Let me pass.

Guard—Have you tae countersign?

Cran—I have.

Guard—Advance then, and give it. [Crandon advances and seizes guard's musket. They struggle.]

Dent—(outside.) Stop him ! Halt, there ! Halt !

[Enter Denton and soldiers. Crandon draws pistol and shoots guard, and as he disappears R. turns and fires at Denton who falls.]

P---Catch the captin, he's hit! (Soldier catches Denton.)

[Quick Curtain.]

ACT III.—SCENE I. PARLOR. MARION SEATED.

Marion—How dreadful a thing is war! And still more dreadful is it when brother is arrayed against brother and father against son. Here am I, a daughter of the South, as nurse to a wounded Northern soldier. But I love the old flag! My father followed it at Buena Vista, and my grandfather fought under it at New Orleans. How could such madness prevail as to seek to destroy the Union? I have friends in both armies seeking daily each other's lives. Where are they to-day? I have not seen Captain Crandon for a year. (Reflects.) I am heartsick of this terrible watching and waiting.

(Enter Maid.) A gentleman to see Miss Kingsley.

Mar—Send him up. (Enter C. L.) Captain Crandon !

Cran—Marion !

Mar—O, Capt. Crandon! What madness brought you here.

Cran—Not madness, Marion. I came to see you.

Mar—But do you not know that discovery here means death to you?

Cran—I face death every day, Marion, and do you think fear of it would prevent me coming to you?

Mar—O, this is dreadful ! If you should be taken ! I cannot bear to think of it.

Cran—Then do not think of it. I am as safe here as anywhere and I intend, with your permission, to remain a short time.

(Bell rings,) Mar—Excuse me a moment. (Exit R.)

Cran—Well, this is rather a cool reception, after a year's absence to come back with my neck in a noose and be called mad. Well, probably it is madness, but it cannot be helped now. (Re-enter Marion.)

Mar—I must say to you Capt. Crandon, that my house is a dangerous place for you just at present.

Cran—In what way, may I inquire? You do not intend to betray me to the Yankees?

Mar—You are unjust; certainly not, but there is a wounded Federal captain here and some of his men come here daily.

You must not be seen by them.

Cran—Who is this captain of whom you seem so careful?

Mar—His name is Denton. He was shot and badly wounded in attempting to capture a man who is suspected of being a spy from the Southern army.

Cran—When did this occur?

Mar—Three days ago, only.

Cran—(Aside.) Ah! Then I did not kill the meddling fool after all. (Aloud.) Is he badly hurt?

Mar—Seriously, but not dangerously, the surgeon says.

Cran—I hardly think it would be quite the thing for me to be seen by these fellows. I suspect that your Captain Denton may blame me for his wound.

Mar—O, do not say that. You surely are not the man for whom the Federals are searching so closely.

Cran—If they are searching for the man who shot your captain, then I am the man.

Mar—O! Heaven!

Cran—Do not fear, Marion. They will scarcely search for the spy at the bedside of the man whom he shot.

Mar—There is one of the Federals who knows you. An Irishman by the name of Carney. He says he met you at your camp down the valley.

Cran—(Aside.) That Irish devil! Then he was the man and that story about his cousin was all made up. He must have recognized me instantly. (Aloud.) Well, it can't be helped now. I'll try to keep out of his way.

Mar—You must not stay. I shall be in agony of dread until I know that you are back among your friends.

Cran—Then it appears that I am not among friends here. This, then, is what I braved the Yankee pickets and took my chances of a disgraceful death to meet?

Mar—You are unkind to charge me with being unfriendly. I am and always will be your friend.

Cran—Yes, I come back after a year's absence in the field

to find you caring for some gallant captain, one of my enemies.

Mar—It is only out of humanity.

Cran—Humanity ! That is not the kind of humanity, I would mete out to these villainous invaders. A long rope and a short shrift would be the humanity I wonld give them.

Mar—Surely you would not take advantage of a wounded man?

Cran—No, certainly not, under ordinary circumstances' But this Captain Denton, if· he lives I will meet again and the next trial my aim will be a sure one.

Mar—O, Captain Crandon. do not say that. I know that the north and south are enemies, but your enmity toward Capt. Denton seems to be a personal one.

Cran---Let him look to it if he ever takes the field again. And you, too, Miss Kingsley. What answer would you make if you were charged with giving aid to the enemies of the south?

Mar—(Rising.) No answer to you, Capt. Crandon. But no one, sir, enemy or friend, who is helpless, can ask assistance at the hand of Marion Kingsley and be denied. I should be unworthy the name of woman, should I refuse.

Cran—O, that's all well enough. But it is very probable that it is a much easier task for you to take care of a handsome captain than it would be were he only a private.

Mar—Captain Crandon, my house is at your service. You will order whatever you require. But you have shown yourself in your true light and I desire to hold no further communication with you. I hope you may return safely to your command. (Exit r.)

Cran—Worse and worse. Capt. Crandon, you may as well go back. You are not wanted here. But Capt. Denton, beware. We'll meet again. And Marion Kingsley will find that there will be a way made to tame her haughty spirit. (Exit L.)

Scene 2. Parlor.

[Denton with arm in sling; Marion sitting near.]

Dent—I did not intend to play eavsedropper, Miss Kingsley, but being unable to get out of hearing, I was an unwilling listener.

Mar—Then you know who my visitor was? O, what shall I do? When will this dreadful war end?

Dent—Soon, I hope. It is dreadful, as you say, and must be doubly so to you, who have friends in both armies.

Mar—What would be the consequences to Captain Crandon should he be taken here?

Dent—The worst, I fear. He is running a fearful risk and more so since Carney recognizes him as the man who boasted that he would penetrate the secrets of our camp.

Mar—If he should be taken, would he be treated as a spy?

Dent—I am sorry to distress you Miss Kingsley, but there would be no other course to take in his case, I fear.

Mar—It would be too horrible. I must see him at once and urge him to forego his desperate undertaking and fly.

Dent—Crandon is a daring man and will, notwithstanding his peril, be wild enough to remain until ae accomplishes his purpose.

Mar—But he must know that everything is against him, being recognized by Carney and yourself, as well.

Dent—It is my unpleasant duty, Miss Kingsley, to endeavor to accomplish his capture, but for your sake I would wish that he would at once leave the camp. I should be sorry were he taken in your house.

Mar—I must see him at once and insist upon his departure. (Exit R.)

Dent—This rebel officer must be more than a friend to Miss Kingsley, notwithstanding her evident kindness to me. I hope he will escape, for the time at least, but if Paddy gets after him he will need to be exceedingly cautious. That green looking Irishman is a regular bloodhound. [Enter Crandon L.]

Cran—Well; you seem to be quite at home here sir. May I inquire why you take advantage of unprotected families to quarter yourself upon them, knowing that your presence is obnoxious to them?

Dent—And may I ask, sir, if I am trespassing upon premises in which you are interested, and if so, why do you leave them unprotected?

Cran—I am interested this far: I take an interest in every household in my country and have a sword to shield them from ruthless invaders, such as you.

Dent—You take care however, to do your shielding at long range. Sir, I am here at the invitation of Miss Kingsley, having been wounded near this place and am at present, her guest.

Cran—That's all very well. I presume that your presence is quite refreshing to the young lady.

Dent—I have no reason to believe that my presence is repugnant to her, and I presume that it is no more refreshing than would be the presence of any man who might be in the condition I am, but I shall trespass upon her kindness but little longer. I take it sir that you areCaptain Crandon of the Confederate army?

Cran—You may take it as you will. I am not here to explain who I am, or for what purpose I came.

Dent—Presuming that you are Capt. Crandon, allow me to say that you are running great hazard in remaining inside our lines.

Cran—Assuming that I am he whom you say, allow me to say that I can take care of myself, even in your camp, and I shall leave it only when it pleases me.

Dent—My advice is given wholly on account of Miss Kingsley. Were it not for her, I should endeavor to compass your capture at once, but for her sake I hope you will take my advice and get away as soon as possible.

Cran—Ah! For her sake you are very kind. Have a care young man. I came in time I see. You with your pallid face and wound, have made fair progress in the good graces of Miss Kingsley, I fancy.

Dent—Sir, if you were a gentleman, you would blush to make such unmanly insinuations, and were I able to stand, I should hold you personally responsible for your language.

Cran—There will come a time. You may thank your wound for safety now, but we will meet again when you cannot urge that plea.

Dent—I have you to thank for my present helpless condition, but it will not be long before I shall be able to be about again, and if you are not hung for a spy in the meantime, I shall take great pleasure in chastising you for your discourteous language.

Cran—You shall not escape. The earth is not broad enough for us both. (Exit R.)

Dent—Well, well; this doughty captain is a very bucaneer. I did not know but he would cut my throat at once. I hope the boys won't get him this time; I would like to meet him on his native heath. (Enter Paddy L.)

Dent—Ah, Paddy, my boy, how goes it to-day?

P—Bad, Captin, bad, an I hope per the same, sor.

Dent—O, I'm on the mend rapidly and expect soon to be out again. But you seem to be downhearted about something. What is it, Paddy?

P—Be dad, Captin, I'm in a quandary.

Dent—Well, what is the quandary?

P—Will sor, its about that divil av a ribil shpy. I've got him safe and sound but I'll be shot if I can foind the shpalpane.

Dent—If you can't find him how have you got him safe and sound? That seems to be a paradox.

P—I'm blisht if I know phat kind of av an ox it is at all.

Dent—Explain yourself, Paddy. Your wits seems to be woolgathering

P—They are, Cap, be dad. But I'll tell yez. That sphy is here some place, but I can't foind him.

Dent—You told me that before. How do you know he is here?

P—Be dad I seen him wid me own eyes.

Dent—Probably he has got away by this time. Do you suppose he would stop here after he knows you recognize him?

P—I do, be dad. Wouldn't he tink we'd tink that by rason av that he'd shkip at wance an that we wouldn't be lookin fur him? An the divil wid jist shtay here because he tinks we tink he's gone.

Dent—That's pretty good logic, Paddy, I must confess. But what makes you think he is here?

P—Because he's here, be dad.

Dent—That is a good reason but how will you prove it?

P—Be dad its proved whin I say it.

Dent—It may be for your satisfaction, but you will have to bring the corpus delicti, as they say in law, before the Colonel will believe you.

P——Phwat's that, now? Be the howly poker, I'll make his corpus kiek high whin I ketch him.

Dent—Yes, when you catch him, Paddy. Bring him around, Paddy, when you get him, I'd like to have a look at him.

P—Look here, Captin, I want to ax yez wan question. Hev yez been out av this room to-day?

Deut—No, Paddy, I have not. Why?

P—Be dad thin, there's more insoide av this house than shows theirselves outsoide av it.

Dent—What do you mean, Paddy?

P—If I didn't say a man standin at wan av thim windys not lang since, thin I'm a Dootchman, an be dad I'll foind out who he is. The young leddy here is the wan he wis comin to say an I belave he's here, be dad.

Dent——Well, if he was here would you take him from the side of his lady?

P—Be dad it wid go hard wid me to bring sorra to the beautiful young leddy, sor, but I'd hev to do it.

Dent——Don't look for him in this house, but keep a guard on the road and at the picket lines. There is plenty of time,

Paddy, understand?

P—I do that same, but he'd better make thracks, sor, be dad. (Exit L.)   [Denton rings bell; re-enter Marion R.]

Dent—Miss Kingsley, my man Carney has seen Captain Crandon at your window. Please to so inform him. I have not betrayed him, but Carney will surround the house with guards in less than an hour and he must be away.

Mar—O, thank you Capt. Denton, he will go at once. (Exit.)

Dent—If he gets away from the house, well; Paddy will take his time. He will probably get away this time, but Paddy will watch him forever.   (Curtain.'

ACT IV.—Scene I. Federal Picket Post.
Sentinel on guard; Soldiers lying about; Song: "Tenting To-Night;" Shot fired R.; picket falls; alarm; Charlie beats long roll; enter rebels led by Crandon; Federals by Denton; Charlie is taken; Federals driven back; Denton springs into rebel rank to rescue Charlie and is taken.

Cran—Secure that man! Don't let him escape on your lives! Take that youngster to the rear, and some of you follow the Yankees a short distance. (To Denton.) Well met, Capt. Denton; I see you have recovered from your wound.

Dent—I have, but I have received a worse one to-day.

Cran—Ah! How is that?

Dent—The capture of that drummer boy.

Cran—Good! I wish that every friend you have were in my hands to-day. I would see that they were cared for.

Dent—Yes, cared for in the way your government is already caring for our wretched prisoners; destroying them by the slow torture of starvation.

Cran—To that torture I will consign your friend, the drummer, but for you, I have determined that you will have no opportunity for escape. Your life is short.

Dent—What would you do?

Cran—Do! Do? I have waited for this moment! To the ignominious death you would have consigned me, had I been taken in your camp, I propose to deliver you, and that right speedily. A rope there, some of you.

Dent—You do not mean to hang me, do you?

Cran—Do I not? Aye, were it the last thing I did on earth, and burned in the bottomless pit to all eternity for doing it, I would hang you.

Dent—You cowardly wretch! I am a prisoner of war. Would you murder me?

Cran—Yes, a thousand times over. The limit of your life is here. You shall not escape me if the devil should come and roar for you.

Dent—Will you permit me to send a message to a friend in camp?

Cran—Not a word. I shall attach a label to your breast when I leave you, which will explain to your brother invaders, who meted out to you your deserts.

Dent—You monster! Proceed. I blush that I should have preferred any request to such a villain.

Cran—Bring that cord and stop the breath of this Yankee marauder! I wish I had a thousand of them.

Paddy—(looking over rock.) O, do yez, be dad?

A rope is brought; Cran. adjusts it about D's neck: soldiers take hold; Paddy looks over rock, attracts D's attention.

Cran—Are you ready there? Up with him.

Stan—(Steps forward and stops men.) By the way, Capt. don't you think you are a little premature about this thing?

Cran—No interference, Stanford! By He who made the world, he dies on the instant.

Stan—How will you report this matter to the Colonel?

Cran—I shall not report it. This is my affair. Stand back!

Stan—I am of the opinion that you had better postpone this thing and turn your prisoner over to the proper authorities.

Cran—Back, Stanford! This is my business: I shall allow no interference. Up with him!

Stan—(Drawing pistols.) Then I'll interfere on my own acconnt. I'll drop the first man that attempts to pull that rope.

Cran—Out of my way Stanford, before I do you a mischief. (Draws.)

Stan—O, put up your artillery, it might go off and hurt you. But I will not stand by and see this man murdered in cold blood.

Cran—Up with him, or by——

Stan—Drop that rope!

[Shots fired; rebs drop rope, pick up guns and look away; Paddy re-appears and motions to Denton who springs up the rock and disappears; Crandon turns to find Denton out of sight.]

Cran—Death and fury! A thousand plagues light upon you! Why did you let him escape? Where is he? Where did he go? Scatter and find him! (Soldiers look about; shot fired; rebels retreat: enter Paddy and Union soldiers, L.

P—O, be the lang handled gridiern, and may the divil toast me fur a shmilt if I wouldn't giv thirtane dollars a month i yez had been here tin minnits sooner. O, be dad! We'd bagged the whole caboodle av thim. Murtherin turf, Captin, but yez wis purty near to glory, me b'y.

Dent—Paddy you are always on hand in time. But I would have willingly submitted to capture if Charlie had been left. Poor boy. And his mother. How can I send such terrible tidings to her?

P—Don't take on so, Captin. We'll thry an get the b'y out av that divil's hole.

Dent—Paddy, I am fearful. That guerrilla Captain will be so enraged at my escape that he will stop short of nothing. I will return to camp. You may remain until I send a relief. Be on your guard. (Exit L.)

P—Won't I be dad, an if that gorilla Captin ever gets in my way again, I hope to be gerrymated if it won't take forty Captin Denton's an a hundred pretty gurls to get him away. (Exit.)

SCENE 2.—PARLOR. MR. & MRS. A. AND ETHEL SEATED.

Mr. A—How heavily falls the rain. I can but think of those who, as we sit by our pleasant firesides, are shelterless to-night.

Mrs. A—I too, but my thoughts go out to our boys in the army. I shudder when I think of my Charlie out in such a storm as this without comfort or shelter.

Mr. A—Yes, mother; I often think of him and his comrades. This would be a comfortless night, surely, lying on the wet earth in soaked garments, or standing a lonely picket in some dreary spot.

Mrs. A—Such a night as this calls to mind the song I have heard the soldiers sing in camp. Do you remember it, Ethel? It commences about the rain.

Ethel—Yes, mamma, I remember it, and will sing it if you and papa will assist me.

Mr. A—With pleasure, daughter. What is the song?

Ethel—It is entitled, " Heavily Falls the Rain." (Sings.) It has been two years since Charlie went away. He must be grown to be quite a man by this time. O, I do wish this cruel war was over.

Mrs. A—I fervently echo the wish, my daughter, but we

must wait God's good time, although it wrings our hearts so terribly.

Mr. A—I believe that the end is near. From what I can gather of news, I am persuaded that the great struggle of the war will take place this summer. Grant in the east and Sherman in the west, will make a mighty effort to break the power of the rebellion.

Mrs. A—May the end come soon, and may my fair haired boy be preserved to me through the storm and perils of war.

(Enter maid with letters, L.)

Mrs. A—Letters, Ethel! O, I hope we may hear good news from Charlie.

Ethel—Here is a letter from Captain Denton, to you, papa, There will be news from Charlie in it, surely. (Mr. A. takes letter and proceeds to read; becomes greatly agitated.)

Ethel—What is it; what is it?

Mr. A—O, my poor lad!

Mrs. A—What is it, husband? In mercy's name do not tell me that my boy is dead.

Mr. A—Not dead. mother, but a------

Mrs. A—Tell me! Tell me!

Mr. A—God help us, mother, our boy is a prisoner to the enemy. (Mrs. A. gives a cry and sinks into chair; Ethel springs to her side.)

Ethel—Dear mother, do not give way so. It may not be so bad. O, my poor brother!

Mrs. A—(Recovering.) Tell me the worst. Let me know it all. O, why did I let my little boy go away from my side!

Mr. A—Captain Denton writes but briefly. He says that in a sudden attack upon one of their outposts, he and Charlie were both captured. Charlie was at once sent to the rear, while he himself was taken into the woods by the rebel officer in charge, and preparations made to hang him, but as they were about to complete their murderous work, he was rescued by our men, led by Paddy Carney. He adds that he will leave nothing undone to secure Charlie's release. Let us hope for the best.

Mrs. A—It is too horrible. I have heard that imprisonment is worse than death, and the thought of my boy, who never before was away from my side, being in the hands of the enemy, breaks my heart.

Mr. A—Take courage, mother. It is the fortune of war. Heaven will temper the wind to the shorn lamb. (Curtain.)

SCENE 3.-- DENTON AND PADDY.

Dent—Paddy, I have sent for you to propose to you a hazardous expedition.

P—A phwat!

Dent—A trip that is attended with great danger & hardship.

P—Is that all. I thought it wis something onhandy.

Dent—Well, it is disagreeable and I am almost tempted to not propose it to you.

P—Shpit it out, Captin, an if there's ony fitin or divarshun in it yez can count on Paddy Carney, be dad.

Dent—Well, there's 'divarshun' in it, and probably some fighting.

P—Out wid it then, an I'm yer man.

Dent—You remember Charlie Aldine, who was captured some time ago?

P—Ah, do I ! He wis a foine little chap an I'd go a linth to do him a good turn.

Dent—I want you to find him.

P—Foind him? Be dad I'll do that same. Where is he, sor?

Dent—That I do not know. He is most likely in some rebel prison.

P—An yez want me to break into that same an git him out?

Dent—Yes, if you can.

P—Be dad I can git in aisy enough; but I'd hev to figger a little to git out, beloike.

Dent—I want you to get into whatever prison he is in and if you can't get him out, stay with him until you are exchanged or the war is over.

P—An so. Captin I'll do it, but if the war is over before

I git ou., yez'll hev to foind me me extra fitin.

Dent—I'll try and do that Paddy. Now, I want to tell you where to go. There is a rebel prison at Cahawba, Alabama, called Castle Morgan; one at Millen, Georgia; one at Andersonville; one at Tyler, Texas; others at Salisbury, Danville and Charleston. You will probably find him at Cahawba, Millen or Andersonville. He may have escaped as I tried to impress upon him the necessity of getting away. You must start to-night. Here is money: use your own discretion about your movements and communicate with me at every opportunity. Good by, and be sure you find the boy. (Exit L.)

P—Well! That's cool onyhow! I'm to foind a b'y loike a nadle in a hay stack. How will I go, be dad? If I wasn't sich a divil of an Irishman, I could be a Dootchman wan day an a F-inchman to-morra. Dootchman, be dad! Lemme thry wance. Nix tur shtay, be gorra! Mox nix ouse, ye divil! Arrah na pogue fur sauer crout und shweitzer case, galore! Be dad, I might pass for a Dootchman in China, but me brogue shticks through me Dootch too much for an American. Frinch! Parley vou Fransay, till yez! Comme il faut, yez son av a tinker! O, be gorra, that's good Frinch if I cud lave aff the bloody Irish. Well, I'll go, but beloike I'd bether go as an Irishman. Me Frinch was neglectid whin I wis in coilig an I'll lit it go. I'll foind the b'y if I bust the Confideracy. I may git me head shot aff, but——)Sings song. Exit R.)

SCENE 4. PARLOR AT HILL'S. HILL, DENT. & CHARLIE.

Hill—Well, young man, you seem to have had a pretty haid time of it. Where have you been?

Char—I was in prison at Cahawba, and because I tried to get out, they sent me away. I escaped at Columbus a week ago, and have been in the woods ever since.

Hill—Its too bad that you did not get through. I wish

we had not stumbled upon you this morning. I will be compelled to send you to Newnan and put you in charge of our authorities there. We will start in a short time. (Enter Stanford and Jordan R.) Good morning, gentlemen, I have a Yankee here that we gathered in this morning while we were out duck shooting.

Stan—(Aside.) Ethel's brother for a million. (Aloud.) What are you going to do with him Captain Hill?

Hill—I'm going to take to Newnan.

Stan—We'll save you the trip, if you like? Jordan and I are now on our way there.

Hill—Just the thing! (To Charlie.) You will go to Newnan with these gentlemen. (Charlie calls Hill aside.)

Char—Captain Hill, I would rather go to Newnan with you. I know these men; they belong to Harvey's scouts and never take Yankee prisoners.

Hill—I will arrange that. (To Stan and Jor.) I shall hold you, Stanford, and your friend, personally responsible for the safe delivery of this young man at Newnan. I shall make inquiry and if he fails to reach there, you shall answer to me.

Stan—No harm shall come to the lad that I can avert.

SCENE 5, JORDAN AND CHARLIE IN THE WOODS.

Jor—I heard you mention the name of Kilpatrick to Captain Hill. What have you to do with him?

Char—I belong to his command.

Jor—You do? Then you are one of that cursed band of raiders, are you?

Char—I belong to Kilpatrick's cavalry.

Jor—(Pointing L.) You go ahead of me. Halt! (Jor. draws revolver, points at Char. who turns his face away for a moment, then throws up his arm and dashes weapon aside.)

Char—You cowardly hound, are you going to shoot me?

Give me one of your revolvers and I will chance my life with both of you.

Jor—I'm going to kill you, you internal raider. You come down here to our country to burn our homes and destroy everything in your way. I never took a Yankee prisoner yet and I won't begin with you. (Raises pistol; Stan. comes up behind.)

Stan—Drop that pistol. What were you about, you fool!

Jor—I am going to kill this Yankee raider.

Stan—Put up your weapon. It does seem to me that some men are born murderers. Now, Jordan, I could put a bullet through you with the greatest of pleasure, although we wear the same uniform, but I would be greatly shocked if you should kill this boy, notwithstanding he is a Yankee. - Strange how some people are constituted, isn't it?

Jor—You keep away from me! I swore I would kill every Yankee raider I got my hands on.

Stan—Well, you had better swear off. Let's argue this thing: Here is a coincidence; I prevented Captain Crandon from hanging a Yankee captain not long since, and he was actually incensed at me. Here I prevent you from killing a boy, and you are ready to spring at my throat. Better drop it.

Jor—I shall not drop it if we fight over it.

Stan—Do you remember what Cap. Hill said about this boy.

Jor—I don't care what Cap. Hill said; I'm going to kill him.

Stan—Now Jordan, I've discussed this matter with you pro and con and you are not convinced. What will prevail upon you to forego the killing of this boy?

Jor—Nothing!

Stan—Nothing? O, by the way then, how is this for an argument? (Shoves pistols in J's face as he turns.) Drop that pistol! Drop it I say! Step aside. It grieves me to have to do this, Jordan. Young man pick up that weapon and hand it to me. Now search that convert of mine for further instruments of warfare. No more? Well. Now Jordan, I am not much on a discussion, but I'm a crack shot, and if you don't like my proced_ ure, some day when the war is over, if you are not hung by that time, I will diseuss the relative accuracy of our respective weapons at ten paces. In order to lighten your load, I'll carry your pistols to Newnan. You may stay behind, but don't get out of reach, I won't trust you out of range. Now young man, I want to give you some advice: You shouldn't go to war. War is a bad thing for young men. It destroys their usefulness and sometimes shortens their lives. You shouldn't have been captured; it is troublesome to our people to have to feed and guard you. You shouldn't run away; you get out among strangers and a person feels comparatively isolated even in the best of company, when that company is made up of those to whom he has not been introduced. Where do you liue when you are at home?

Char—At Morena, Illinois.

Stan—Yes! Your father's name is ——

Char—Phillip Aldine.

Stan—You have a——! Well, we'll not go further. It is ad form to pry into family secrets. You tried to get away, did you?

Char—Yes, I did, and I'll try again if I get an opportunity.

Stan—Perfectly proper, if you succeed; but I would strongly advise against it unless you do succeed. I would hardly try it if I were you, until I got outside of the Confederate lines. But what I was going to say; I expect to go north shortly and it would probably be a great comfort to your mother to know that you are alive and well and hopeful.

Char—O, yes, indeed! I wish that I could let her know that I am living.

Stan—Well, I will give you some more advice. Don't try to get away at hresent. Be patient. The war is nearly over. Don't get homesick. I will write to your mother and tell her that you will pull through. We are almost at Newnan. Close up, Jordan, we have reached our destination. (Exit L.)

Scene 6. Parlor. Marion and Stanford Seated.

Stan—You are intending to go north, Miss Kingsley, I understand?

Mar—Yes. There is nothing left here for me to do and I have relatives in one of the western states. I will remain with them, at least until the war is over.

Stan—I am somewhat acquainted with your uncle's family and as I have business in that section, I may do myself the honor of calling upon you, with your permission, when, as you say, "the war is over."

Mar—I should be pleased to have you call, Capt. Stanford.

Stan—May I inquire how soon you expect to start, and is there anything I can assist you in?

Mar—Thank you. I will start in a few days. My preparations are all made so far as relates to matters here. I will have to obtain permission at the Federal outposts to travel north, I suppose, but could hardly ask you to obtain that permission for me.

Stan—I should be delighted to obtain that permission for you, but I am afraid my preference of the request would lead you as well as myself into difficulty.

Mar—Yes, therefore I will not lay the task upon you trusting to find gentlemen among the Federal soldiers.

Stan—That I can vouch for, Miss Kingsley.

[Enter servant L.] A gentleman to see Miss Kingsley.

Mar—Show him in. (Enter Crandon L.) Capt. Crandon!

Cran—Miss Kingsley I am delighted to see you in health.

Stan—Howdy, Crandon?

Cran—Ah, Stanford, you here? I thought you were with your command.

Stan—Excuse me, Capt, but our thoughts of each other run in the same channel. We are both mistaken, it seems.

Cran—I learn, Miss Kingsley, that you have decided to go north?

Mar—I have so decided Captain Crandon.

Cran—Allow me to say that I consider your decision both ill-timed and unwise.

Mar—Pardon me, Capt. Crandon, but I am of the contrary opinion. I have relatives in the north who will be glad, I know, to have me with them.

Cran—But your duty to the south. You should not leave now, when the arm of every man and the heart of every woman is needed to secure the victory.

Mar—Captain Crandon, I love the south, but this whole country is my country. I am opposed to secession and am horror-stricken at the suffering and desolation its mad projectors have brought upon us.

Cran—This is rank treason.

Mar—Well, if it is, I can only say with our illustrious forefather; "If this is treason, make the most of it."

Cran—This is not a light matter, Miss Kingsley, as you will find. What will protect your property if you are absent?

Mar—My negroes have been pronounced free by President Lincoln. My land cannot be destroyed or carried away. What other property I had has been taken by the Confederate government to aid as you say, the south in securing victory.

Cran—You shall not be allowed to leave here. Who knows but that you may carry information to th Federal armies?

Stan—Crandon, allow me to remind you that Miss Kingsley is not to be suspected of playing the spy. That is left for such as yourself.

Mar—You may be able to delay my departure, Captain Crandon, but I believe those who know me best would never impute to me the charge you hint at.

Cran—Well, I shall not be responsible for the safety of your property here. My men, even now, are not easily persuaded that you are not in full sympathy with the north, especially since you cared so unselfishly for that gallant Yankee Captain who was afterwards saved from his just deserts by our mutual friend, Stanford, here.

Mar—Sir!

Stan—By the way, Crandon, I am totally averse to discussion, so far as I am concerned, but your attitude toward Miss Kingsley requires some consideration from me. I never quarrel in the presence of ladies. Miss Kingsley will excuse us for a few minutes, I am sure.

Cran—Miss Kingsley has no need of your championship.

Stan—True, quite true, where it is a matter between sha and you, Crandon.

Cran—Then sir, you can take your leave.

Stan—When? To-morrow? I'll think of it.

Mar—Captain Stanford is in my house, sir, and he leaves only at his own pleasure.

Cran—O, he does! Another Captain attached to the charming Miss Kingsley's chariot!

Stan—Miss Kingsley, I sincerely beg your pardon for this unseemly disturbance in your presence, but really the case demands it. (Bows, then walks Crandon out R. by the collar.)

Cran—Unhand me villain, or I'll do you a mischief.

Stan—(Returning.) Miss Kingsley you will excuse me a moment. I am desirous of seeing Capt. Crandon briefly before he goes.

Mar—O, Captain Stanford, do not go. I am afraid there will be blood spilled.

Stan—No, Miss Kingsles, I assnre you. (A s he bows.) Not to-day. (As he Exits R.) But very likely to-morrow.

Mar—Another proof of the lawlessness of war. I am afraid that something dreadful will happen. Captain Crandon is so dreadfully passionate and Captain Stanford will take no pains to mollify him. O, there will be murder done and how can I prevent it. (Re-enter Stanford R.)

Mar—O, Captain Stanford, what have you done?

Stan—Unfortunately, Miss Kingsley, nothing. We had no mutual friends to see the affair, and I was afraid that if I fell there would be no one to show that it was fairly done, the matter has been dropped. (Aside.) For the present.

Mar—O, I'm so glad. But I am sorry Captain Crandon has such a high temper.

Stan—So am I, indeed, and I would not be surprised if he himself was sorry in a short time.

Mar—Do you think he will try to prevent my going north?

Stan—I might do him injustice were I to say he would. I am inclined, however, to believe that he will not. I think that he will be reasonable when I next meet him.

Mar—I hope so, indeed.

Stan—Well, Miss Kingsley, I have already overstayed my time, and must go, but before going, may I be allowed to ask you one question?

Mar—A dozen, if you wish, Captain Stanford.

Stan—One will suffice. If by fortune or misfortune I should survive the war and other vicissitudes, when I come north will I be welcomé at your uncle's home?

Mar—I can speak for uncle Aldine. I am sure you will be welcome.

Stan—I am not at this moment asking a welcome from uncle Aldine. You will be there if I come. How may I expect to be received?

Mar—(Turning aside but giving her hand.) You will be welcome. (Exit R.)

Stan—I have followed the fortunes of this Southern phantasmagoria for four years and this is the end. The end of the phantasy. It was only a wild dream of ambition; dreamed by a few, for their own aggrandizement. The dreamers looked forward to power and honor, but they sought it at the expense of honor and power. They precipitated this whole country into a wanton, wicked and woful war, the burden of which fell upon the common people. And what have they gained? A lost cause! Blood; blood on every hand. Crime, woe, want, death. The curse of Egypt is over us; there is one dead in every house. Burning cities, ruined homes, desolation, despair! The brand of Cain is on every brow, and the righteous blood of our brother Abel cries out from the thirsty ground. Passions engendered which no ties of kindred or friendship can reconcile or tame. What a page in history! I have lost the capricious friendship of Crandon, for preventing the murder of that Yankee captain. Well, if I have done one good act in all my checkered life, I am glad of it. He was jealous of the Yankee and wanted to get rid of him. Crandon is a hot-headed boor and Denton has a girl in the north. He does not know that Miss Kingsley is Ethel's cousin, and he does not suspect that I am the college senior who graduated when he was a junior. Well, let us live life slowly. We can have what we want, if we will only wait for it. I believe I have an element of fairness in my make-up and must needs cultivate it. I have received satisfaction at the hands of Miss Kingsley ; now I must go and give satisfaction to my friend Crandon for so unceremoniously kicking him down stairs. I regretted the occurrence on Miss Kingsley's account, but Crandon was served better than he deserved. I suppose he will want blood for it. Well, I'll try and let him have some of his own. (Exit L.)

SCENE 7—THE DUEL IN THE WOODS.

(Enter Crandon, his Second and Surgeon R. Stanford, Second L. Seconds greet each other and the Surgeon.)

Stan—Ah, doctor, you brought the necessary appliances, I perceive!

Dr—Certainly; certainly. (Rubbing his hands.) All in excellent shape, too, Captain.

Stan—Doubtless !

Cran's Second—The arrangements are these : Principal's at six paces. The word, one two, three; fire! One, stop! Take your places, gentlemen. (Cran. and Stan. assume positions.) My principal says he is willing to receive an apology and let the matter rest.

Stan's Second—My principal says it is too late. Go on and give the word. Are you ready, gentlemen?

Cran's Second—One, two, three, fire! One, stop! (Cran. stands unharmed. Stan. clasps his left arm to his side.)

Stan's Second—Are you hit, Captain, you are pale!

Stan—Not a word. Load and fire again.

Second—But Captain, you—

Stan—Silence. I'll kill him if he had shot me through heart. Be quick about it. (Pistols loaded, principals in places.]

Cran's Second—Are you ready gentlemen?

Stan's Second—One, two, three, fire! One, stop.

(Crandon staggers and is caught by second and is lain down. Surgeon feels pulse. Stanford and his second advances)

Curtain.,

.

ACT V.—Scene i. Prison.

(Denton in foreground. Charlie lying down in front. Other prisoners lying around.)

Dent—My search is ended. And this—this is what I find. Here is the boy I took from his father's rooftree and his mother's fostering care—an inmate of this festering prison house. Where sleeps the vengeance of God, that this place should batten on human beings? All! all!—the strong in their strength, the youth in their bloom dropping into this rotten mouth of death. This is

4

-but let its   ...   .ccurse forever on the earth. The true history of th   ...   wil startle and shock the world with a tale of horror, of ... and death heretofore unheard of and unkown. No pen will ... describe, no painter ever sketch, no imagination comprehend its fearful and unutterable iniquity. It seems as if the concentrated madness of earth and hell had found its final lodgment in the breasts of those who inaugurated the rebellion, and that this prison had been selected for the most terrible human sacrifice which the world has ever seen. Into these narrow confines are crowded thirty thousand enlisted men of the Union army, many of them the bravest and best, and the most heroic of these grand armies which carried the Stars and Stripes to victory. For long and weary months here they suffer, are murdered, and die. Here they linger unsheltered from the heat of a tropical sun by day, and drenching and deadly dews by night: in every stage of mental and physical disease; hungered, emaciated and starving. Festering with unhealed wounds, gnawed by the ravages of scurvy and gangrene, with swollen limbs and covered with vermin they have no power to extirpate. Exposed to flooding rains which drove them drowning from the miserable holes in which, like swine they burrowed. Parched with thirst, and mad with hunger, racked with pain, or prostrated with the weakness of dissolution; filthy with smoke and mud; with naked limbs and matted hair, eaten by the gnawing worms which their own wounds engender; with no bed but the earth, and no covering but the clouds and weeping sky; these men, these heroes, born in the image of God, thus crouching and writhing in this terrible torture and sickening barbarity will stand forth in history as a monument of the surpassing horrors of Andersonville as it will yet be seen and read in all future time, fitting counterpart of Dante's Inferno or Milton's hell. Thus I find my boy—yet unsubdued, but failing day by day. How could I tell this tale of horror to the loving mother and gentle sister. Hope ? Aye ! Let us hope. (Goes to Charlie.) Charlie, boy, keep up your courage, I believe we are near the end.

Char—(Looking up.) It has been a long time, Horace, but I am going to pull through. I believe I can outlive the Confederacy even if I only get a pint of meal a day.

Dent—You aie a brave lad, Charlie. We'll se the end together. Let us give the boys a song. (Sing Tramp, Tramp, Tramp. Invisible chorus. Enter Paddy R.)

Dent—Paddy Carney !

P—Who's that? O! phat the div-- O! by the bones ot St. Pathrick, if it isn't the Captin!

Dent—Yes, Paddy, it is I or what's l ft of me.

P—Be, dad its moighty little that's left of yez.

Dent.--- Starved, Paddy, starved in this hapless prison.

P---Stharved, d'ye say? An me wid lashins av grub. 'Here be dad?---(Hands D a cracker.)----Ate yer fill av that. I've got a paice av another

Dent---Thank you Paddy; but here's one that must have the first.--(Goes to Charley.)

Paddy---Who's that? The Charlie boy? O! blissid St Peter! An are yez found? O! glory and smoke!---(Goes to Charley.)---Hillo, Charley boy. Hi! d'ye mind this! Hooray lad! wake up. Here's yer Irish mither and faather, be dad.

Char.---O! Paddy, is that you? Have you come to take me home?

Paddy---Be dad, I have that same. Git up! We'll have lashins to ate in a jiffy an may de divil fly away wid de ribels.

Dent— When I was captured they took all my money and valuables and I have had to live on prison rations now for two months. Have you any money?

P—Money? I'm a millionaire, but yez needn't tell ennybody. I'll go and git sum grub if there's any to be had in this divil's galosh. (Exit R.)

Dent—Cheer up Charlie. Paddy will bring us something to eat shortly, and we'll have everything that this God-forsaken place affords.

Char—I feel better already, Horace, and if I can have

only half enough to eat, I'll pull through.

Dent—Well, we'll have it my boy. [Enter Paddy with a haversack of crackers..)

Paddy—Here be dad, ate till yez bursht. I med a dicker wid a bloody reb to bring us sum swate peraties to-night, an be jabbers we'll hev a faste that'll startle yez. Hooray fer Tipper-a-ry an down vid the traitors an oop wid the shtars. The bloody wa-ar is over, beloike, an we'll be goin home wan av these days.

[Tableau.   Curtain.]

ACT VI.—Marion seated.

Mar—The long war is over at last. The soldiers are re-turning home. Those of the north wreathed in glory; those of the south with heavy hearts for their bitter defeat. But grief, deep and lasting mingles with the joy of the north and the bitterness of the south. Breaking hearts for the graves on every hillside, and in every valley of the south. Despair for the noble boys, whose souls went up to God from Libby's dismal prison, and the burning sands of Andersonville. O, what a terrible reckoning there will be with the madmen who plunged our beautiful country into such dreadful woe. O, my sunny southern home, my heart goes back to you to-day. But where are the friends who were with me there only a year ago? Crandon, Denton, Stanford. Shall I ever see them again? And where is Charlie? Dear cousin Charlie! It is now a month since the surrender of Lee, and still no word from the lost. Aunt Aldine suffersin silence, but I see that she is failing day by day. Oh, heaven send back to her her noble boy, to cheer her breaking heart. (Sings "The Blue and the Grey.")

Enter Mrs. A. and Ethel L.

Mrs. A—I heard you singing, Marion. I wish I could sing, but my heart is too heavy with sorrow for that.

Mar—O, aunt, I wish I could do or say something that would lighten your sorrow, but I can only say, Hope !

Mrs. A—I do hope, Marion, but I dare not think of what will come when I must cease even to do that. (Sits down overcome. Marion retires weeping.)

Ethel—Mother dear, keep up your courage. I believe Charlie will yet come home. (Enter Stanford L.)

Mrs. A—Mr. Stanford !

Stan—The very same, Mrs. Aldine. A little more staid, perhaps, than when you knew me years ago. And this is Ethel without doubt. But how grown ! Well years work wonders. (Greets Ethel.) I met Mr. Aldine on the way from the station. He was going to the postoffice, he said.

Mrs. A—Yes, the good news of Lee's surrender comes to us with sadness. We hoped when the war closed we would hear of our boy, but have heard nothing yet.

Stan—Did you get my letter, Mrs. Aldine, written some time since about the lad ?

Mrs. A—We did, Mr. Stanford, and you have our grateful thanks for the hope it gave us.

Stan—I believe that my words will come true, Mrs. Aldine. Charlie is of that nature to bear up under difficulties. [Enter Mar.] Ah ! Marion ! (Advances.)

Mar—Captain Stanford ! (Greeting. Enter Mr. A.)

Mr. A—Good news, children ! Good news !

Mrs. A—O, Charlie ?

Mr. A—Yes, Charlie. Here's his letter from Jacksonville, Florida. Three weeks on the way. Thank God ! The boy is safe.

Ethel—What does it say, Papa ? Read it.

Mr. A—(Reading.) After the surrender of Lee, the Johnnies took us out of prison and brought us down to Florida and turned us loose in the woods twenty miles from this place, telling us to follow the railroad track and it would take us to our lines. We needed no second bidding. It was a long walk, but we kept up, and on the morning of the 29th of April Capt. Denton, Paddy Carney and myself sighted the old flag at Jacksonville, pretty poor in flesh and short of clothes, but the happiest fellows in the world. He closes by saying that he won't be far behind the letter.

Ethel—Papa, you are hiding something from us, I can see it in your eyes. What is it?

Mr. A.—Don't be inquisitive, Ethel! Let us take the news easily. Mother, you will see your boy before long.

Mrs. A.—And I will be so happy.

Mr. A.—[Going to door.]—Come in boys.—]Enter Charley, who goes to his mother· and Dent., who goes to Ethel and greeting. Enter Paddy.]

P.—O, be dad! Here we are. The prodigies have returned. Give us a gould ring and a new gown.—[They form a half circle Mr. A left. Mrs. A. Charlie, Dent., Ethel, Stan., Mar., Paddy.]

Mrs. A.—O, Charley, how you have grown!

Char.—Well, mother, I did as well as I could for the chance I got. We didn't live very high while boarding with the Johnnies.—[Paddy laying off in dumb show to Stanford.]

Mr. A.—Peace has returned to our country and our hearts.

Ethel.—Let us sing our peace song.—[Mr. and Mrs. A. C., D., E., S., M., G. and Paddy in front; others behind. Song.—" 'Tis Finished." Solo and chorus. Curtain.]